THE LORD OF THE RINGS

MOVIE TRILOGY ™

COLORING BOOK

First published in 2016 by
Harper Design
An Imprint of HarperCollins*Publishers*
195 Broadway
New York, NY 10007
Tel: (212) 207-7000
Fax: 855-746-6023
harperdesign@harpercollins.com
www.hc.com

This edition distributed throughout the United States by:
HarperCollins*Publishers*
195 Broadway
New York, NY 10007

ISBN: 978-0-06-256148-0

First Printing, 2016

Printed and bound in the United States of America.

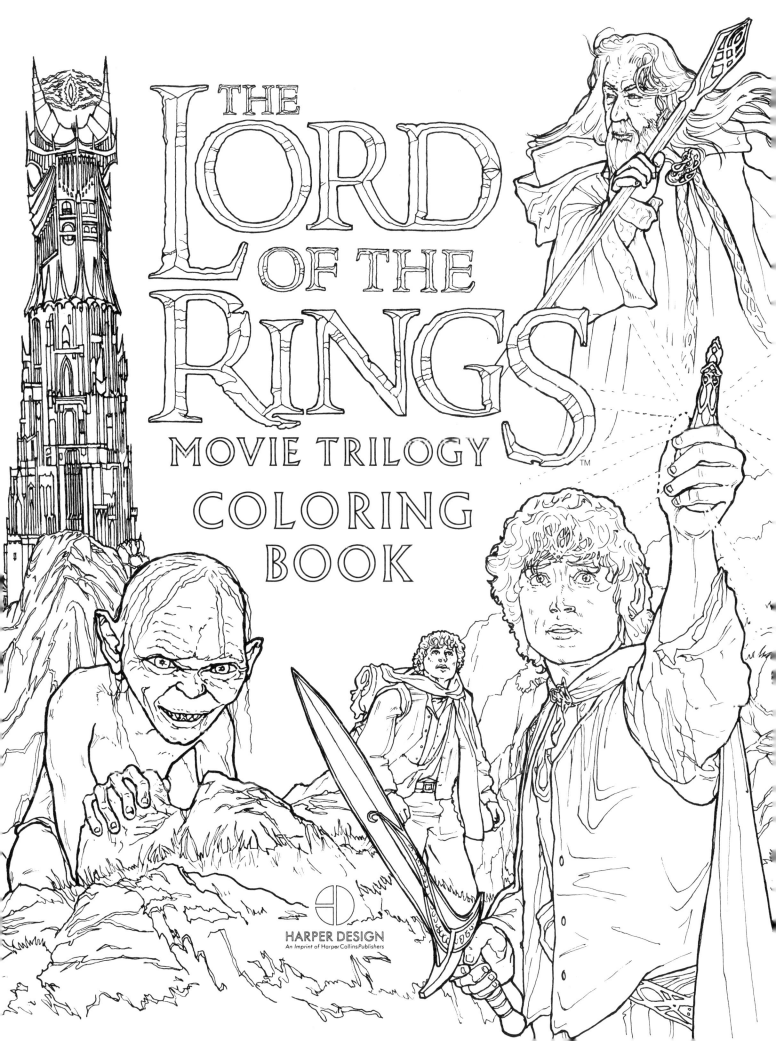

INTRODUCTION

When Frodo Baggins steps out of Hobbiton on his quest to deliver the One Ring to a place of safety, he has no idea where the journey will take him and his companions: from the magical Elven realms of Rivendell and Lothlórien to the abandoned Dwarven kingdom of Moria; from the wizard Saruman's stronghold at Isengard to Rohan, land of the Horse-lords; from the fortress at Helm's Deep to Minas Tirith, the kingdom of the proud men of Gondor; from the overrun city of Osgiliath to the battlefields of Pelennor; from Cirith Ungol and the Nazgûl's Tower of Sorcery at Minas Morgul into the very heart of Mordor. Along the way our heroes encounter Elves and Ents, Uruk-hai and Orcs, the Haradrim and their towering war-elephants, the Mûmakil, the monstrous spider, Shelob, and the pitiful Gollum, who has deadly ambitions of his own.

The many characters, creatures and strange lands of Middle-earth encountered by the Fellowship of the Ring in their epic journey have captured the imagination of book readers for more than 60 years. And when *The Lord of the Rings* movie trilogy exploded on to the big screen in 2001, the films dazzled moviegoers young and old, bringing the stories to life in a way no one had believed possible. As well as the exciting scripts, powerful acting and immersive music score, it was the visual feast that made the films so special—painstaking production design, authentic craftsmanship and spectacular New Zealand locations, all adding up to films that were full of life and color.

This coloring book invites you to celebrate the film-makers' achievements and take your own exciting, artistic journey through Middle-earth. Whether you want to color each image true to life or prefer to add your own imaginative flourish, the choice is up to you!

'I've thought of an ending for my book.

"And he lived happily ever after, to the end of his days."'

Bilbo

Frodo

'I will take the ring to Mordor!'

'Anyways, you need people of intelligence on this sort of ... mission ... quest ... thing.'

Pippin

Arwen

'If you want him,
come and claim him!'

Aragorn

'If by my life or death
I can protect you, I will.

You have my sword.'

'. . . AND MY AXE!'

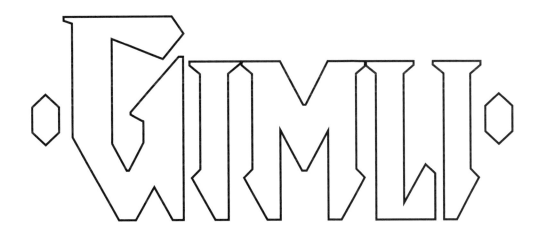

GIMLI

'You shall not pass!'

Gandalf

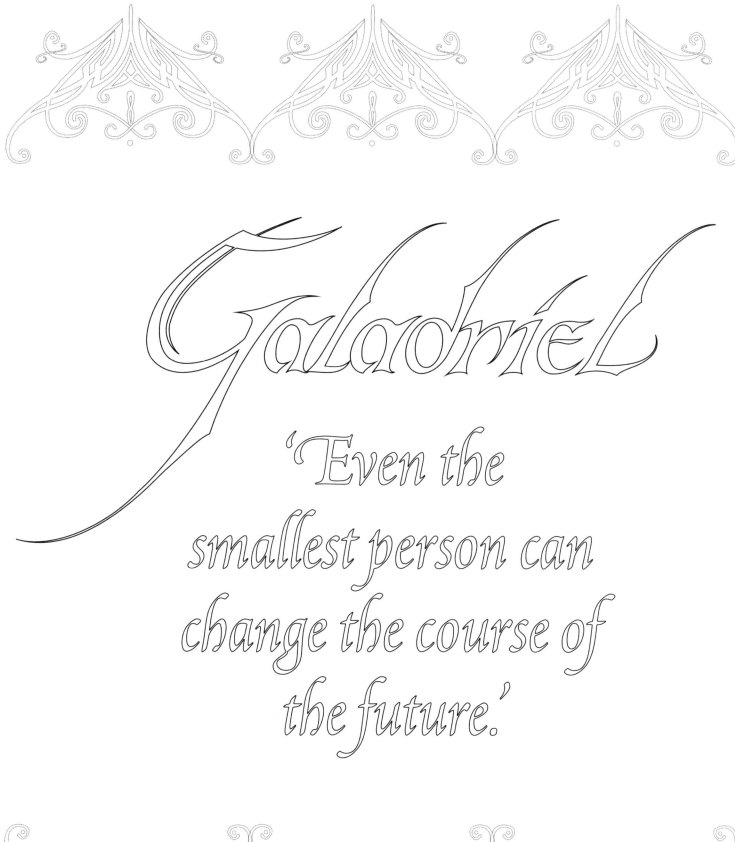

Galadriel

'Even the smallest person can change the course of the future.'

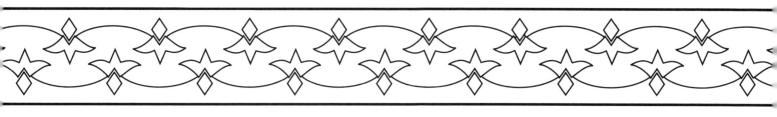

'It is a strange fate
that we should suffer
so much fear and
doubt over so small
a thing.'

BOROMIR

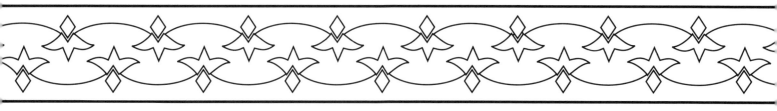

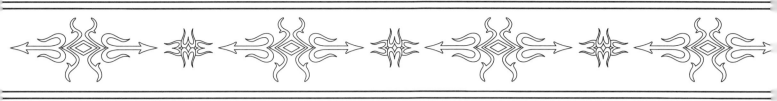

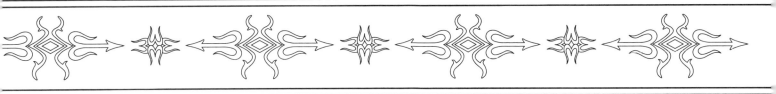

Merry

'I think we might have made a mistake leaving the Shire, Pippin.'

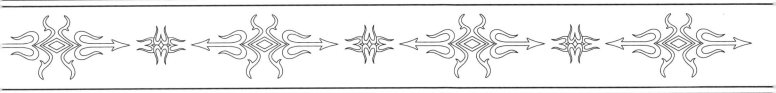

'We wants it, we needs it.
Must have the precious.
They stole it from us.
Sneaky little hobbitses.
Wicked, tricksy, false!'

Gollum

'The stars are veiled.
Something stirs in the East.
A sleepless malice. The eye of
the enemy is moving.'

Sämwise

'Let him go!'

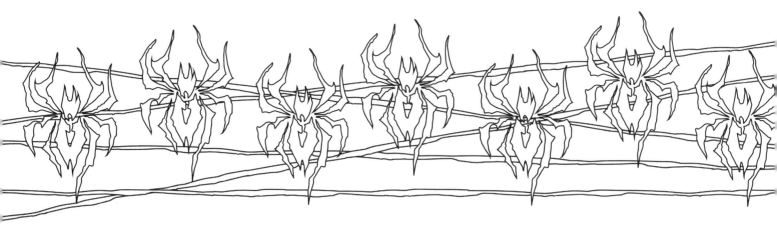

Éowyn

'I Am No Man!'

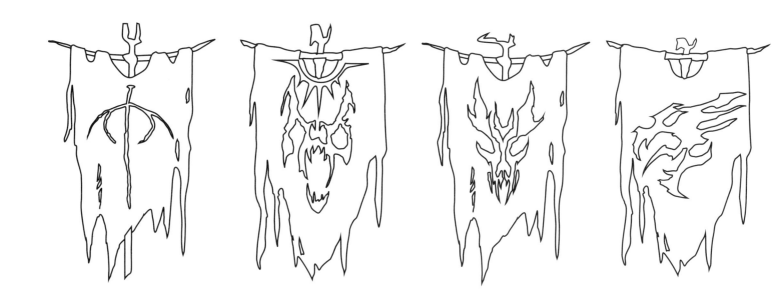

'Ten thousand Orcs
now stand between
Frodo and
Mount Doom.'

Gandalf

Sämwise

'Come on, Mr Frodo.
I can't carry it for you …
But I can carry you!'

'This day does not belong to one man but to all. Let us together rebuild this world that we may share in the days of peace.'